THE PARTY

Barbara Reid

Scholastic Canada Ltd.
Toronto New York London Auckland Sydney
Mexico City New Delhi Hong Kong Buenos Aires

To absent friends.

The illustrations for this book were made with Plasticine
that is shaped and pressed onto illustration board.
Acrylic paint and other materials are used for special effects.

Photography by Ian Crysler.

Scholastic Canada Ltd.
604 King Street West, Toronto, Ontario M5V 1E1, Canada

Scholastic Inc.
557 Broadway, New York, NY 10012, USA

Scholastic Australia Pty Limited
PO Box 579, Gosford, NSW 2250, Australia

Scholastic New Zealand Limited
Private Bag 94407, Greenmount, Auckland, New Zealand

Scholastic Children's Books
Euston House, 24 Eversholt Street, London NW1 1DB, UK

Library and Archives Canada Cataloguing in Publication
Reid, Barbara, 1957-
The party / written and illustrated by Barbara Reid.
ISBN 978-1-4431-1309-0
I. Title.
PS8585.E4484P37 2012   jC813'.54   C2011-905483-3

6 5 4 3 2 1   Printed in Singapore 46   12 13 14 15 16

Me and my sister
all dressed up to go.

Today is the day of the party.

Our friends are out playing.
We had to say no.
We're on our way to the party.

We are stuffed in the car
with a cooler,
some chairs,
a bowl full of dip
and a tin full of squares.

3

Squirmy and shy
by the end of the ride,
we take a deep breath
and step inside . . . .

"Here you are! Come on in!
Look how you've grown!"
There's no way to miss
being kissed by Aunt Joan.

6

The very worst part of the party.

People pile in.
More kissing. More fuss.
We look at the other kids.
They look at us.

How do we start at the party?

"I cut my own hair," Claire begins.
"Mummy cried."
Sally has stitches:
"I flew off the slide!"
Ben lost a tooth
when his launcher derailed.
Kate split her lip
'cause her parachute failed.
We all claim our fame at the party.

"Want to play sharks?" Danny asks.
Yes we do!
"I'll be It. If I catch you,
then you're a shark too!"

The lawnchairs are lifeboats,
the grass is all water.
Kate leaps to the birdbath —
too late! Danny's got her.
We're all in the game at the party.

I zip through the crowd
with the sharks on my tail.
Spring to the deck:
"Up anchor! Set sail!"
Then a tidal wave washes us all out to sea,
and the only survivors are Simon and me,
hiding deep in the hedge at the party.

15

Safe in our hideout
we're planning a raid.
Slip past the dragon —
we're not afraid.

Then slowly, so slowly,
on tiptoe we creep . . .
Reach for the treasure chest:
"Now! He's asleep!"
Steal away to the edge of the party.

They call us: "Come eat!"
In a minute — we're busy!

We're spinning in circles
until we get dizzy.
We laugh till it hurts at the party.

But . . .
there's sausage rolls,
casseroles,
pineapple rings.
Devilled eggs,
chicken legs,
little cheese things.
Salads with jelly,
salads with beans.
Enough? Let the dog
lick your party plate clean.
Leave room for dessert at the party.

Happy Birthday to you!
My favourite song.
Happy Birthday to you!
Put your party hat on!

Happy Birthday, Dear Gran,
"Make a wish!" we all shout.
Happy Birthday to you!
And we blow them all out.
We all give a cheer at the party.

Gran cuts the cake.
"Step right up, get your share!"
We make an escape
under Uncle John's chair.

In our kids-only party tent,
no one will mind us.
Licking off candles,
we toss them behind us.
We are kings under here at the party.

The night air invites us
to enter the race —
a galloping wide-open heart-thumping chase!
Lopsided cartwheels collide in the air.
We all fall down giddy
with grass in our hair.

Then Ben says, "Look out!"
and I signal the others.
It's time to play hide-and-go-seek
from our mothers!

27

It's way past our bedtime.
The streetlights are on.
We load up the car
and we try not to yawn.
Oh, what a great time,
what a wonderful time,
such a very late time
at the party.